Hi Everyone

I've been so busy with all my horses this year that I haven't had a lot of time for writing. But I'm delighted to be back with four brand new stories about Tilly and her beloved horse, Magic Spirit. My new stories will all focus on Tilly and Magic's partnership as they work together and compete at a higher level. Tilly's way of riding reflects my own way of riding. The advice that Tilly is given is what I would teach from my past experiences, and it's also how I've been taught. Over my career it's what I have found has worked for me as I've competed with my horses, so I hope you find it useful, but most of all I hope you will enjoy reading Tilly and Magic's new adventures as much as I have enjoyed writing them.

Keep reading, keep riding and follow your dreams!

See you soon.

Coming soon

Team Training

Team Work

Team Magic

Out now

Magic Spirit

Red Admiral

Rosie

Samson

Lucky Chance

Solo

Pride and Joy

Neptune

Parkview Pickle

Nimrod

Moonshadow

Autumn Glory

Goliath

Buttons

Rusty

Royal Flame

Stripy

Free Spirit

Tilly's Horse, Magic

Team Spirit

Pippa Funnell

Orion
Children's Books

First published in Great Britain in 2014
by Orion Children's Books
a division of the Orion Publishing Group Ltd
Orion House
5 Upper St Martin's Lane
London WC2H 9EA
An Hachette Livre UK Company

1 3 5 7 9 8 6 4 2

A catalogue record for this book is
available from the British Library.

ISBN 978 1 4440 1198 2

www.orionbooks.co.uk

Printed and bound by CPI Group (UK) Ltd, Croydon, CR0 4YY

For Anna Nolan,
my niece and
goddaughter

Chapter One

'If you find a certain type of fence difficult,' said Angela, 'don't avoid it. You never know when you'll have to face it at a competition.'

She was standing in the middle of the sand school helping Tilly with her stunning grey, Magic Spirit. Tilly looked back at the combination jump she'd just tried: three fences in a row, with one or two strides between each. So close, Tilly thought, that there was hardly enough room between them to land from one, and take off again for the next. They'd done several Pony Club events, nearly all successfully, but Magic's eagerness to do the job had caused a few problems in the show jumping phase. He was fine with single fences and okay with doubles, but he'd developed a habit of getting too quick down the combinations. And as a result he sometimes had one, more often two parts of it down.

Tilly shifted uncomfortably in her saddle.

'Tilly,' called Angela as she rebuilt the fences, 'don't wriggle! Sit quiet with your seat.'

Tilly was convinced Angela had eyes in the back of her head. How had she seen that? How many times had she told Tilly to sit quiet and still?

She could feel herself tighten up as she approached the combination. As Tilly tightened, Magic tensed too. She was so relieved that she had met the first element on a good stride, that she pushed him forwards. He reacted instantly by rushing, skimming worriedly over the first part, just about leaving it up, getting faster all the time, hitting the second and completely destroying the last element.

'Don't panic, just come again more quietly. Be careful on your approach not to be steadying him with the hand, yet pushing and driving him with your seat,' said Angela. 'It's sending mixed messages to him.'

Tilly did what Angela said and immediately Magic approached in a more relaxed way. She'd given him that bit more time to jump the first element so he landed in better balance to clear the next two parts without rushing.

'Wow, that made such a difference,' said Tilly, beaming. 'I wish it was that easy at a competition.'

'It will be, you just have to keep working at it. Remember Magic really trusts you. Every day I watch you training, I see you improving.'

Tilly smiled. Angela was right. No matter how tricky the Pony Club Eventing Area Competitions were becoming, she and Magic would rise to the challenge – and they'd do it together. Apart from this small problem, they'd had a good season so far and were hoping to be selected for the Open Pony Club

Championships. Tilly gave Magic a pat and praised him for trying. He lifted his head and half-turned to look at Tilly, letting her know that if she rode him correctly he would try his best.

Not everyone could get such an affectionate response from him. The regulars at Silver Shoe Farm, where Tilly stabled Magic – including the vet, the farrier and various experienced stable-hands – described him as a horse who knew his own mind. And when they weren't feeling quite so generous, they used words like stubborn, quirky, and difficult.

Tilly's experience of Magic, however, had always been different. She was the one person he always behaved for, the one person he trusted. That bond had started the moment they'd caught sight of each other on a busy road in Tilly's home town, North Cosford. Tilly had found him abandoned and running loose while she was out with her mum. He was a danger to road-users and himself. Despite the fact that her only experience with horses had been gazing at pictures in *Pony* magazine and dreaming of owning a champion eventer, Tilly hadn't hesitated. It never crossed her mind that this desperately thin, highly strung, wild-looking horse, who was obviously very distressed, could possibly harm her in any way. Every time anyone had tried to approach him, he reared, striking out with his front legs. He was confused and terrified. Bizarrely, Tilly managed to calm him by being quiet and non-threatening, yet confident and reassuring, talking to him all the time. The crowd around them, including Tilly's mum, couldn't believe what they were seeing, the extraordinary trust that the horse was putting into this quiet girl. So when Angela, Silver Shoe Farm's owner, had arrived on the scene and agreed to take him on, she agreed to take Tilly on too. With years of top eventing experience behind her, Angela knew that a bond like that between a horse and person was truly special.

Horses, eventing and helping at Silver Shoe Farm were Tilly's life. Her friend Becky said she lived on Planet Pony. She did the normal things too. School. Homework. Catching up with friends. But most of all, horses were her whole world. While her school friends gossiped about movies and make-up, she thought about snaffle bits and cross country fences. While they whispered about boys – boys they had crushes on, boys in the dinner queue, boys on television – she daydreamed of winning Badminton. When they talked about 'falling in love at first sight' (Becky seemed to at least three times a day!), Tilly simply thought about the deep and limitless feelings she had for Magic. Planet Pony all the way.

As Tilly wandered back to the yard with Magic, she thought about Angela's advice. What was the problem with the combination? It wasn't the height or width of the fences. She and Magic had cleared way bigger jumps. In fact, they were known for their courage. Perhaps it was the technical complexity? Perhaps it was the fact that most times they'd jumped a combination before, they'd messed it up? A fear of failure, a crisis of confidence. But Tilly knew confidence was vital in such a demanding sport as eventing. She remembered something her half-brother, Brook, also a talented young rider, had once said: 'Believe in yourself and your horse will believe in you.'

'That's it,' she said as she tied Magic up in the wash-down area. 'Combinations may be our nemesis, but we're not going to let them get in our way. They're not going to stop us from making the team. We'll conquer them somehow.'

Tilly took a breath and thought of the progress she'd made. When she'd first started riding, she'd had passion and natural flair, but that was it. No experience. No knowledge, apart from the hints and tips she'd picked up from websites and books. But she'd never had the chance to try them out. Over the last few years, however, with Angela teaching her, she'd developed new skills. She had worked tirelessly on the basics: riding without stirrups to help with her balance, making herself ride with her hands together, so she learned to steer and straighten with her legs. Often when her friends were going off on hacks, she would be repeating more transitions, and getting circles exactly the size she wanted, without falling in or out. Now she and Magic had a genuine shot at success.

Despite their obvious potential, it hadn't been a straightforward journey. Tilly knew in her heart that if she'd never rescued Magic from that roadside, she probably wouldn't be in the saddle at all. There was no way her adoptive parents, the Redbrows, could afford the upkeep of a horse. Riding lessons were expensive enough, never mind the stabling costs. Thankfully, Angela had agreed to cover Magic's upkeep, everything from hay to farrier's and vet's fees, and she had given Tilly riding lessons in exchange for working in the yard. She'd told Tilly and her parents countless times that it was worth her while, because she could see how amazing their partnership was.

But at Pony Club competitions, the fact that Tilly didn't officially own Magic sometimes made her feel out of place. She'd meet riders with fantastic horses, state-of-the-art-horseboxes and all the latest tack and equipment and she'd wish she had the same. Worst of all though, was her fear that, one day, Magic could be taken from her. Technically, he still belonged to someone else. She only hoped that someone would never want him back.

Angela always insisted it didn't matter whether a rider had every bit of tack and equipment going, whether they had luxury stables in their own back garden, or the money to buy five top competition horses. Trust, dedication and talent were everything. And since Tilly and Magic had plenty of all three, they deserved a chance.

Thinking about chances, Tilly stroked Magic's neck and stared at the horizon, across the spring green of the trees and fields to the rolling hills. Just as she was about to start brushing him down, her phone buzzed. She gave a small sigh and answered it.

'Tilly?' said a voice. 'It's Penny from North Cosford Pony Club.'

'Oh, hi, Penny. How are you?'

'Great, thanks. And I think you will be too, when I tell you why I'm calling. We've been reviewing the North Cosford Branch Event Team, Tilly, and you've been selected. That's right. You're going to the championships.'

'*What*?'

Tilly gasped, covering her mouth with her hand. The smile burst out of her.

'I *am*?'

'Of course. You must have known that you and Magic were in with a chance. This year you've been one of our most successful partnerships.'

'But I thought because of my hiccups in the show jumping . . .'

'You've still had better results than most,' Penny interrupted. 'And besides, we're sure that under Angela's watchful eye you're working on that issue.'

'Oh, wow!' said Tilly. 'Totally, totally wow!'

Chapter Two

Three days later, Tilly was smartening up Magic in the yard, and getting him ready to meet the rest of the team at Penny's farm, which Tilly knew well. It was where all the North Cosford Pony Club rallies were held. She brushed his coat, picked out his hooves and took extra care with his mane, rolling and carefully sewing up each plait. At Silver Shoe, she was considered to be a 'plaiting expert' and was often called upon when horses were being groomed for shows and competitions. She didn't mind. It was a pleasure to be able to help make them look beautiful.

Tilly had already been told the names of the three other riders on the team. She'd met two of them before at competitions: Anna Carson and her Connemara cross thoroughbred gelding called Matinee, who was consistent and reliable at all times; Ben Lye-Jones, the only boy on the team, and his father's Irish hunter aptly named The Hedgehunter, because he loved jumping hedges. He was as laid back as his jockey. The only name Tilly didn't recognise was Kya Mackensie. She wondered if Anna or Ben knew anything about her.

Penny's farm was only a short distance from Silver Shoe, so Tilly hacked there. It was a bright day and she enjoyed riding down the tree-lined lane, onto the bridle path that crossed the village green. She couldn't wait to see her team mates. In fact, as she turned into the driveway to Penny's farm, her stomach danced with butterflies.

As soon as she reached the main yard, Ben popped his head out of one of the stables.

'Hey, Tilly. Hey, Magic.'

'Hi, Ben.'

'How cool is *this*? We're going to the championships!'

Tilly dismounted.

'I know,' she said. 'Can you believe it? I was so surprised when I got the phone call.'

Ben looked at her.

'Really? But you're the obvious choice. Everyone's been talking about you, Little Miss Whisperer, and your "magic" Magic. You're one of Penny's rising stars.'

Tilly blushed.

'It's me that's the surprise,' he said. 'Penny's always moaning at me for not taking competitions seriously enough, so I was amazed when I got picked. I guess she wants to give me a chance to prove myself . . .'

'And use your talent,' said Tilly.

'What talent?' said a voice from behind them.

It was Anna.

'Hello, shorty,' said Ben, as he ruffled Anna's bob. 'I see you made it too.'

Anna smiled and poked him in the ribs. Tilly

could tell that beneath the banter, they were close friends, which was a good sign.

Anna turned to Tilly.

'Please don't talk to Ben about being talented,' she said. 'It'll only go to his head – which is already stuffed with ego!'

'*Moi*? Ego?' said Ben, with a grin.

'I'm glad you two get along, said Tilly. 'This is going to be fun.'

'Yes,' said Anna, rolling her eyes. 'Just as long as my nightmare mum doesn't get involved.'

Tilly knew Anna's mum from Pony Club events. She was a regular, known for shouting and arguing and generally trying to take over. There were always a few pushy parents at Pony Club, but she was one of the infamous ones – the total opposite of Anna, who seemed playful and easy-going.

'Is your mum here today?' asked Tilly.

'She drove me and Matinee over in the trailer. She wanted to hang around, but I managed to convince her to go shopping. She's browsing the farm shops looking for organic vegetables.

She's got this new thing, that in order to have competitive edge, I'm only allowed to eat healthy food. No chips. No pizza. No cola. It's so boring, it's untrue.'

'And what next?' said Ben. 'Is she planning to ban Matinee from eating polos?'

'Probably,' said Anna.

'How is Matinee?' said Tilly, remembering the consistent dun. She'd watched him jump a few weeks ago. For a compact horse he had a huge, scopey jump.

'He's great. I was just about to unload him from the trailer when I saw you arriving. How's Magic? His coat is so shiny!'

She reached out to stroke Magic's nose. She did it calmly, obviously at ease interacting with horses. Nonetheless, Magic flicked his head and stepped away. He didn't want to play.

'Is he shy?' said Anna.

'He's just . . . Magic,' said Tilly. 'He's got a habit of being cagey around unfamiliar people.'

'Oh yeah,' said Ben. 'I remember seeing you guys at the Areas. One of the judges tried to put a rosette on his bridle and he practically stampeded, until you stepped in, and he was fine again. Sounds like he's a "one horse/one rider" kind of boy.'

'That's definitely him,' said Tilly, secretly feeling proud.

The bond she had with Magic meant more to her than anything. And it was another good reason for Angela to let her ride him. If *she* didn't, no one else would be able to. Everyone at Silver Shoe Farm had had problems with him, even Angela and her head lad, Duncan. They'd all been bucked off, ignored, pushed into fences and found him a real quirky rogue at times. But with Tilly, Magic was a different horse.

'So do you reckon we're the winning team?' asked Ben, a gleam in his eye.

Tilly held her breath, feeling hope crackle inside her.

'We should certainly give it a go,' she said.

'All the way to the championships,' said Anna.

'What about Kya Mackensie?' said Tilly. 'Is she here yet? Have either of you met her?'

Ben and Anna glanced at each other.

'We've met her once,' said Anna, but the look on her face made Tilly uneasy.

'Right. Great. What's she like?'

'She moved to Cosford a month ago,' said Ben. 'Apparently, her dad's been travelling a lot for work, so she's lived all over the world. She has a seriously smart horse called Bastion. He's a very flash-looking Dutch warm blood, who used to be ridden by a top event rider, but was too slow and not quite quick-thinking enough for the highest-level competitions. Even so he's been round some big events. You've got to see him. He's incredible. Must have cost a fortune. And she's a major talent, which is why she's been picked for the team. It's just–'

'What? What is it?'

'Let's just say she's . . . *confident*.'

'Yes, confident is a good word,' said Anna. 'Better than mega-tastically arrogant anyway.'

Magic twitched. Tilly soothed him with a tickle, then stared at Ben and Anna.

'Are you saying she's–'

'High maintenance? Yes.'

'Put it this way,' said Anna, 'she makes my mum look like a chilled tortoise. To be honest, we weren't too happy when we heard she was the fourth team member.'

Tilly frowned. This wasn't good news. An impressive horse and talented rider were important, but high maintenance wasn't something the team needed. Tilly had worked so hard to get to this point, the last thing she wanted was some stroppy *prima donna* causing problems. She heaved a sigh and hoped that Ben and Anna were wrong.

Just then, an enormous, glossy, silver horse box pulled up.

'Here we go,' said Anna. 'Talk of the devil.'

'Devil?' said Ben, with a wink. 'I wouldn't go that far . . . *yet*.'

To Tilly's relief, the devil, aka Kya Mackensie, turned out to be a pretty, petite fourteen-year-old, with immaculate ice-blonde straight hair. As soon as she saw the three of them standing in the yard, she burst into a smile.

'Hola! Look at you guys! My team! You're going to be my team! How brilliant is this?'

She ran forward and hugged them all. Three kisses on each cheek and an admiring gasp when she came to Magic.

'Wow! What a horse! Is he yours?'

Tilly nodded.

'Meet Magic Spirit,' she said.

'Cute name. What is he?'

'Um – he's a bit of a mix actually.'

'Pure-bred though, right?'

She raised her hand to stroke Magic's nose. He backed away.

'Don't worry,' said Tilly. 'He does that to everyone.'

'Sure,' said Kya. 'I know how it is. Bastion's a Dutch warm blood. And he's *such* a snob. Honestly, I'm certain he actually thinks he's a fashionista. Like, he only greets people who wear Jack Wills.'

She tossed her ice-blonde hair back and laughed, then turned to Ben and Anna.

'Oh guys,' she said. Her accent had a distinct transatlantic twang – the result, Tilly assumed, of her speaking different languages while her dad worked abroad. 'I'm so tired! I was seizing up in the front of the cab the whole way here. Those seats are so small. What's the deal? Is our lesson straight away or can I stop and get a drink and stretch out for a bit? I've got my yoga mat with me.'

Ben raised an eyebrow.

'I know, *sad* isn't it? I take it everywhere I go. But I tell you what, it's so good for you. Personally, I had great posture before, but since yoga, it's *amazing* – and the difference that makes to your balance when you're doing dressage and jumping decent fences . . . you'll see what I mean.'

Tilly smiled and blinked, surprised and pleased by Kya's effusiveness. She definitely had an air about her, a whiff of pampered luxury, but she was bubbly too – and ambitious. If she was doing things like yoga to improve her riding posture, she obviously took competing seriously, which could only be a good thing. As Tilly watched her chatting to Ben and Anna, her worries abated. She gazed at her new teammate and admired her polished riding boots, her Ariat jodhpurs and her Toggi waistcoat. It was hard not to be impressed. In fact, the more Tilly studied her, the more eager she was to get to know her. And even more eager to meet Bastion, who was lucky enough to command a brand new four-horse lorry.

Chapter Three

Tilly knew that to succeed at the championships they needed to practise everything, from accuracy in their dressage to show jumping technique, to cross country stamina. The effort didn't bother her of course – any excuse to ride Magic. She was delighted when Angela suggested she should invite the team over to Silver Shoe Farm at the weekend to run through their dressage test. They only had a few weeks till the big day.

On Saturday, Tilly moved the jumps out of the indoor arena, then she and Duncan downloaded the championship dressage test from the Pony Club website and read it through. There was nothing too demanding – working trots, serpentines, medium trots, changing reins, circles, halts and salutes. The challenge was in making sure all these movements were carried out accurately with balance, rhythm and suppleness – and without clicking or using the voice.

Kya was the first to arrive. Bastion walked into the yard as if he owned the place. His glossy chestnut coat had a slight white spotting on the upper legs and belly. There was no doubt that he had competed to a high level and had been correctly ridden because he was built up in all the right places. He had a very good top line – well-muscled on the top of his neck and over his quarters.

Kya jumped down and removed her high-vis jacket.

'Hola, Tilly. It's wonderful of Angela to allow us to use her facilities. So, what's on the agenda?'

'Dressage,' said Tilly.

'Oh, I love dressage. Last winter when I was

living in Switzerland, Bastion and I won sixteen rosettes. But I expect you've won a few dressage rosettes too?'

Tilly smiled. She preferred the pace and thrill of the cross country. Dressage was her least favourite discipline – which is why she wanted to practise it.

Tilly collected Magic from his stable and she and Kya waited patiently for Ben and Anna to arrive.

'It's okay, boy,' said Tilly as Magic pulled a face at Bastion. 'Bastion is a friend, a team member. We have to get on with our team mates.'

She smiled at Kya. Kya smiled back.

'We can wait here for the others,' said Tilly. 'I told them to get here for nine.'

She glanced at her watch. Quarter past already.

'I'm sure they'll get here soon.'

'So, tell me a bit more about Magic?' said Kya. 'Where did you find such a beautiful horse?'

'Good question,' said Tilly, smiling to hide

her awkwardness. 'He . . . um . . . we . . . um . . . we kind of found each other.'

Kya looked puzzled.

'At a stud farm, you mean? Did you have him bred especially? I'm guessing he's got sport horse genes?'

Tilly looked at the sky, then at Magic.

'I like to think he's got some wild Mustang in him, far back in his breeding,' she said, thinking about her trip to the Kentucky Horse Trials, where she'd groomed for Angela, who was competing with her horse, Pride and Joy.

While she was there, she'd met a magnificent Mustang called Free Spirit, who had reminded her of Magic. She'd also learned that her birth mum, who'd died soon after she was born, had lived and worked on a Native American reserve, looking after a herd of wild Mustangs, and that she and Brook undoubtedly had a Native American father who'd made amazing horsehair bracelets. Tilly wore three horsehair bracelets of her own. She'd made two of them herself – one from Magic Spirit's tail and one from a zebra foal called Stripy. The third, the original, had been given to her by her mum. Tilly's connection to the Native American tribe had made her realise that her natural way with horses wasn't just a coincidence. It was in her blood.

She wasn't sure whether to explain all this to Kya though. She was proud of her newly discovered heritage, but it was complicated and personal – and it wasn't exactly the standard Pony Club life story. She briefly recounted the story of how she'd been orphaned, then adopted by the Redbrows, how she'd dreamed about riding but had never thought she'd be able to, then all at once, had come across Magic and been reunited with her half-brother, Brook. Kya was fascinated, mainly about Magic.

'You seriously don't know who his sire was?' she probed. 'I can tell you Bastion's background. His sire was Hengeld, twice winner of the Rotterdam Cup, and his dam belonged to a member of the Danish royal family. But Magic?

I mean, you want to go all the way to the top, right? You have to know your horse can take you there and is bred for the job.'

'Magic will definitely take me there,' said Tilly.

'I like your confidence,' said Kya. 'But you must have some idea? It'll tell you everything you need to know on his passport, his documents?'

'Um . . . I don't have his passport.'

Kya raised her eyebrows.

'The truth is,' Tilly said warily and before she could stop herself, 'I don't officially "own" him. I rescued him. When no one came forward to claim him, Angela, the owner at Silver Shoe, had no option but to keep him. Magic and I developed a bond immediately. He was difficult with other people, but for some reason he stayed calm around me, so Angela said I could help produce him in exchange for working at the yard, because we couldn't afford . . . *Anyway*, she saw our potential and gave us some training and now, here we are. Please don't tell anyone though. I'm trying to keep it quiet. I'm scared his owners will find out how well he's doing and ask for him back.'

'Sure,' said Kya. 'I can keep a secret. But what a sweet story. I guess he's a bit of a mystery horse. Well, I hope it works out for you both.'

'Thanks,' said Tilly. 'Me too.'

She looked across at Magic. When he saw he had her attention, he pricked his ears and whickered, then bowed his head and nuzzled her shoulder.

'He obviously adores you,' said Kya.

Just then, Tilly's friend, Mia, came over.

'Hi,' she said, eyeing Kya.

Tilly introduced them. Mia was a Silver Shoe regular and one of Tilly's closest friends. She'd known her for ages, from the days of her very first riding lesson when they'd shared a pony called Rosie. Mia now had her own horse, a fine chestnut called Autumn Glory and the girls often rode together. In fact, Mia knew everything about Tilly and had seen first-hand the way her relationship with Magic had developed.

'We were just saying how much Magic Spirit clearly loves Tilly,' said Kya.

'Oh, yes,' said Mia. 'They're inseparable. Like best friends. Always have been.'

She nudged Tilly in the ribs.

'You know this is Silver Shoe Farm's number-one horse whisperer. If anyone's got a problem with their steed, they just need to talk to Tilly. Honestly, she's got such a knack. It's awesome. Horses are drawn to her. Not just Magic, all horses . . . but especially Magic.'

Tilly blushed.

'Yes, it's exactly the same for me and Bastion,' said Kya. 'Whenever I'm around he makes *such* a fuss. He doesn't care about anyone else. Just me. It's the secret of competition success, don't you think, Tilly? The bond between horse and rider.'

'Definitely,' said Tilly.

She was pleased to hear Kya say this, that they shared the same beliefs about horses. She'd practically forgotten Ben and Anna's warning about Kya's attitude and snootiness.

Mia smiled.

'Is that your horse, then?' she said, nodding to Bastion. 'He's gorgeous, isn't he?'

'Yes,' said Kya. 'He's competed all over Europe with his former jockey. You must have heard of Matty Taylor? He's a well-known rider, but he felt Bastion was ready to downgrade and be sold as a horse for a junior. He does well. I've jumped him all over the world.'

'And now you've landed up in North Cosford. Lucky you. Are you starting at our school?'

'Cavendish Hall, actually.'

'Yes, of course you are,' said Mia, glancing at Tilly.

Cavendish Hall was the exclusive boarding school on the other side of town, where students had their own stable block. Brook and his horse, Solo, were there, and the girls had ridden over to see him a few times.

'Can I give him a pat?' Mia asked Kya.

Mia stepped closer to Bastion, but he flattened his ears in an unfriendly way.

'Like I said, he only responds to me.' Kya

reached up to rub Bastion's nose, but he shook his head and pulled a grumpy face.

'That's so weird. He must be nervous,' Kya said, embarrassed. 'He's never usually like this. Maybe it's the new surroundings. Or maybe it's you, Mia.'

'Or maybe it's Tilly . . .'

They both turned to see that Bastion had moved closer to Tilly and had started nibbling at her hands, sniffing her treasured horsehair bracelets, his ears pricked forward. Tilly patted his nose and quietly greeted him, then stepped back. Bastion followed. He seemed intent on getting Tilly's attention. Now, Kya didn't just look embarrassed. She looked annoyed too.

'Sorry,' said Tilly, flustered. 'He probably thinks I've got mints or something. '

'You're so modest, Tilly,' said Mia. 'You know it's because of your whispery thing.'

She looked at Kya, then back at Tilly.

'Well, I'll leave you two to get on with your training,' she said. 'I promised Duncan I'd help with a delivery of hay. What are you going to work on today?'

'Dressage,' said Tilly.

'Enjoy,' said Mia. 'Just you two?'

Tilly glanced at her watch again.

'No,' she said. 'Our team mates, Ben and Anna, are supposed to be here. Where on earth are they? I've only got the indoor arena for an hour.'

'Lateness drives me mad,' said Kya. 'It's so unprofessional. I tell you, they'd better not show up late on competition day. I won't be having it.'

'I *bet* you won't,' said Mia.

Chapter Four

Ben and Anna finally turned up, half an hour late, in a horsebox driven by Anna's mum. Ben jumped out and darted into the yard.

'Sorry, sorry, sorry we're late,' he said. 'It's my fault. I couldn't find all my stuff.'

His phone rang.

'Sorry. It's my girlfriend. Do you mind if I take this?'

He turned away to answer his phone. Tilly and Kya glanced at each other.

'*Not* impressed,' muttered Kya.

Anna came storming towards them, a scowl

on her face. Her mum was close behind.

'Anna!' she shouted. 'Stop when I'm talking to you! Listen to me!'

Anna marched on. It was obvious they were having an argument. Never mind the two horses still in the horsebox. All Tilly and Kya could do was watch.

'I've had enough of your behaviour, young lady,' snapped Anna's mum. 'The championships are less than two weeks away. If you don't start showing more of a commitment to your riding, I'll take your phone off you–'

'*So*?' said Anna. 'Just stop going on at me, all right?'

She ran over to Tilly and Kya, as though they could protect her from her furious mum.

'Save me,' she whispered. 'My mum is unbelievably annoying when she's like this.'

Tilly and Kya stood up tall and tried to smile at Anna's mum.

'Hello, Mrs Carson,' said Tilly.

'Hello, girls,' Anna's mum huffed. 'I'm just trying to tell Anna what an honour it is to get picked for the team. Don't you agree? She needs to work if she wants to succeed.'

'Yes,' said Kya. 'Most definitely.'

Suddenly Angela, who'd heard the shouting, came over.

'Hi,' she said, greeting Anna's mum. 'Welcome to Silver Shoe. So exciting about the championships, isn't it? I think these four will make a great team. They could do very well.'

Angela looked back at Tilly, gave her a knowing smile, and then took Anna's mum by the arm.

'I guess we should leave the girls to unload the horses,' she said, leading her away. 'Why don't you and I go and have a cup of tea in the clubroom? I promised I'd spend some time watching their dressage and giving them tips, but there's time for a chat. I want to hear all about your daughter and her horse.'

Good old Angela. She always knew how to solve a problem. With Anna's mum out of the way, they could now concentrate on training.

At least Tilly *hoped* they could. It wasn't the best of starts.

When Ben finally got off the phone, he and Anna unloaded their horses, Hunter and Matinee, and tied them up to the side of the lorry. Ben offered them both a drink while Anna took their travel boots and rugs off, then they got them tacked up ready for their dressage lesson.

'I've tied Magic up so I can give you a hand,' said Tilly, approaching.

'Thanks,' replied Anna, giving Tilly a set of exercise boots to put on Matinee's legs for protection.

'What about Hunter?' Tilly asked.

'No thanks, I never bother with boots,' said Ben.

'What if Hunter knocks into himself at a crucial time? It could prevent him from going to the championships,' said Tilly, concerned.

'He's survived four years jumping big hedges

in the hunting field with my father and without boots, so hopefully he can look after himself trotting round an indoor arena doing boring old dressage,' said Ben.

He was a typical boy. He loved the thrill of galloping and jumping but found going round in circles rather dull.

'Talking about boots, I need to borrow some for my own feet,' he added. He'd picked up his father's instead of his own in his hurry to get ready.

'I think there might be a spare pair knocking about in the tack room. Hopefully, they'll fit you. Follow me,' said Tilly.

They left Kya and Anna to warm up their horses, and crossed the yard to the tack room.

'Are you usually this laid-back?' said Tilly.

'Uh, yeah. It's kind of what I'm known for. That and being late. Oops.'

Tilly smiled, but inside the tension wriggled. She didn't want anything to jeopardise her chances of success. She knew how important it was to her to be organised and well turned out.

If Ben was this disorganised and distracted in competition, it could ruin things.

'Here we go,' she said, pulling a pair of Duncan's old boots from the shelf. 'Try these.'

Ben kicked off his Converses and slipped his feet in.

'They're massive,' he said. 'But they'll do. Don't look so worried, Tilly. I may be scatty, but I know how to ride.'

Tilly shrugged. 'I hope so,' she said.

As they walked Magic and Hunter to the indoor arena, she asked about Anna.

'What were they rowing about?'

'Oh, it's a daily occurrence with those two. Always the same old thing. Anna's mum wants Anna to be this perfect little Pony Club princess, while Anna would rather be playing bass in her band.'

'She's in a band?'

'Yeah. A girl band. They're really good. They do gigs and stuff. Trouble is, band practice and horses don't mix.'

'But she's such a talented rider!'

'She knows that,' said Ben. 'And she totally loves Matinee. It's not that she doesn't want to ride. She just doesn't want the pressure of constant competing. She wants to spend time on her music.'

'Hence the arguments.'

'Exactly. Her mum hates the music thing. Her only aim in life is for her daughter to become a top event rider. She's forever on her case. And it's only going to get worse now they've made it to the champs.'

Tilly nodded as she listened to Ben. As much as she felt for Anna, she knew Anna's reluctance to compete could be yet another obstacle to her championship dream. It didn't look good: one who was disorganised and one who wasn't keen. At least Kya seemed to have the required drive and focus.

The four horses, Magic, Matinee, Hunter and, of course, beautiful Bastion, shared none of their riders' issues and doubts. They'd accepted one another. They didn't have to worry about each other's personalities. They stood close together, whickering and swishing their tails.

'Come on then,' said Tilly. 'Let's make the most of the time we've got left.'

They joined Anna and Kya and warmed their horses up at walk, trot and canter on each rein, working on their positions at the same time, until they felt they were ready to ride through the dressage test.

'I trust you all know the correct dressage test?' Tilly asked, looking at Ben and sensing what the answer would be.

'Ah, um . . .'

'You're hopeless,' sad Kya and Anna at exactly the same time.

'I'll only go through it once, so memorise it, then you can watch us ride. You can go last.'

Luckily, Tilly had the printout in her pocket. She started reading.

'A. Enter at working trot and proceed down the centre line without halting. C. Track right. B. Circle right, fifteen metres diameter. Give and retake the inner rein on the first half of the circle.'

Halfway through, Ben's phone rang again.

'Uh, sorry guys, it's my girlfriend again. I've got to take this.'

He jumped off, handed Hunter's reins to Anna and walked away with his phone pressed to his ear. Tilly clenched her jaw, trying to remain calm. Kya sucked her cheeks in.

'Does he want to win or not?' she hissed.

'Go easy on him,' said Anna. 'He and his girlfriend are just about breaking up. He's pretty stressed. He needs to sort things out.'

Kya sniffed.

'He can sort things out in his own time. Not mine. I'm going first.'

Without further delay, she trotted down the centre line as Tilly and Anna watched. They went through the test effortlessly. Bastion's movements were elegant and graceful, yet with a workman-like quality. He looked regal. And Kya looked like a queen. Tilly was impressed by Kya's concentration and accuracy. It had been a little awkward before, when Bastion had responded to Tilly in the yard rather than Kya, but clearly Kya knew what she was doing when it came to dressage.

'Sorry I'm so late, guys,' said Angela, entering the school.

'You've just missed Kya do her test, but we can vouch that it was pretty cool,' said Tilly.

Anna and Matinee's dressage test was less polished to say the least. They wobbled down the centre line, which wouldn't give a good first impression to a judge. As Anna gave away her inside rein Matinee rudely shoved his head up in the air. Lots of small costly mistakes.

'All of you must remember not to go throwing away marks unnecessarily with silly inaccuracies. Ride to your markers. If it says 'trot at letter A' then trot at A, not two strides before or after. And that fifteen-metre circle needs to be fifteen metres, not thirteen or seventeen,' Angela said as she watched Anna.

Tilly and Magic showed what sort of expressive work they were capable of, but got a bit carried away in medium trot. Tilly got too brave, asked too much, resulting in Magic breaking into a canter. He also anticipated in his walk. As Tilly started to shorten her reins in the free walk on the long rein, he jogged for a couple of strides.

'Except for those couple of mistakes, it's getting better, but not there yet,' Angela told her. 'Remember to keep your right leg on in the halt, because he always swings his bottom to the right.'

Tilly had lost count of the number of times Angela had told her that.

'Just one more thing,' said Angela.

'I know. I used my voice,' said Tilly, frustrated.

She knew if she wasn't careful she would get two penalties for using her voice.

'I find it so difficult. I talk to Magic without realising it.'

Having listened to Angela's feedback, Ben's test was almost as perfect as Kya's – even though he wasn't one hundred per cent sure exactly where he was going. Somehow he found his way. Tilly remembered his comment. '*I might be scatty, but I can ride.*'

To her relief, he could.

Early that evening, Tilly was getting a drink in the clubhouse, when Mia came in.

'How did it go today?'

'Good. In the end.'

'And how's your new BFF?'

'You mean Kya?'

Mia nodded and twiddled her horsehair bracelet. The one Tilly had made for her from Autumn Glory's tail. She nodded. 'And let's not forget her *amazing* event horse, Bastion.'

Tilly gave Mia a look.

'Do I get the impression you're a teensy bit jealous?'

Mia shook her head.

'No. It's just . . . I've got a funny feeling about her, that's all. I know she's your new team mate and everything, but . . . when you get bad vibes it's hard to shake them off.'

'Oh, Mia. Kya's *fine*. Don't be down on her.

I know she seems a bit flash and fabtastic. But she's really nice, trust me.'

'I trust *you*,' said Mia. 'Anyway, I can't stop. I've got to go and see if Autumn is settled. Then Mum's picking me up. See you.'

She gave Tilly a quick hug, then turned and walked out, leaving Tilly staring, wondering.

Chapter Five

The following weekend, the team agreed to meet at a show jumping competition half an hour away. Not only was it a chance for Tilly to work on her jumping, but it was also the last chance for them to get together as a team before the championships.

Kya had offered to give Tilly and Magic a lift in her fantastic brand-new horsebox. She arrived early that morning. Her mum drove the lorry into the yard where Tilly and Magic were waiting. Kya hopped out of the cab, full of smiles and energy. Tilly couldn't help but admire her immaculate cream Ariat breeches. Tilly was wearing her old favourites – a pair of beige jodhpurs her mum had bought her – and she carried a tweed jacket that used to belong to Angela. Her clothes were smart, but still, she had to admit, they were a little old and faded, as if they'd been in the wash a few too many times.

'Thanks for the lift,' said Tilly.

'No problem,' said Kya. 'There's room for four horses in here. We might as well make use of it.'

'Isn't it hard work for your mum driving such a big lorry, especially in some of the narrow lanes?'

'Sometimes. But do you know what makes it worth it?' She gave Tilly a twinkly-eyed grin. 'When you get to a competition and everyone stops to admire you. In a vehicle this big, people assume you're important. See for yourself.'

Tilly walked Magic round the back of the lorry and up the ramp. Magic hesitated. He hadn't travelled in such a large or luxurious vehicle before. Tilly tied him up and gave him a small haynet to travel with.

'See you at the showground,' she whispered, giving him a reassuring pat. 'Enjoy travelling in style.'

Sure enough, when they pulled into the showground where there were horseboxes and trailers of all shapes and sizes parked in neat rows, people stopped and pointed, or simply gazed in awe. Tilly giggled.

'It's like we're famous,' she said.

'I know,' said Kya. 'Fun isn't it?'

But fun as it was, neither of the girls wanted to forget the very serious business of practising for the championships. As soon as they arrived, they dropped the ramp, and unloaded the horses. Tilly went to tie Magic up to the side of the lorry.

'You can't do that,' exclaimed Kya's mum, in a horrified voice. 'He could scratch my beautiful paintwork. We have a special padded plastic sheet that fixes to the side, I'll put that up and then you can tie both horses up to the side, before you offer them some water.'

The girls made their way over to the secretary's office, to enter the one metre open.

'I wonder where the others are. What's the betting Ben has forgotten something important?' said Kya.

As they wandered over to the ring to watch the last few competitors jump in the class before theirs, Tilly suddenly spotted Ben, leading Hunter towards them.

'How are we going to change him?' asked Kya, referring to Ben, who was on the phone yet again.

'I don't think we are, or I'm not sure whether we should. That's just the way he is, as long as he gets the results, who are we to say he is wrong?'

They both watched as he ambled over, leading Hunter, who looked scruffy with his badly plaited mane. As he got to them Ben hung up and put his phone back into his pocket.

'Hi,' he said.

'What have you done to Hunter's mane?' asked Kya.

'I was in a hurry,' said Ben. 'I ran out of time.'

Tilly gave Hunter a pat.

'Poor thing,' she whispered.

Close up she could see what a rushed job Ben had done. Fine for now, but she knew she would have to help Ben get himself and Hunter smartened up for the championships. It's one thing to be laid back and relaxed about life, but another being this sloppy and messy, thought Tilly.

Ben went to the collecting ring steward to see which order they were jumping in, while Tilly and Kya went to get Magic and Bastion.

'You're first,' said Ben to Tilly as she rode into the collecting ring on rather a keen-looking Magic, who was thrilled to be at another competition. They were like parties to him.

'Then it's me, then Kya and Anna last.'

'Talking of Anna,' said Kya, 'where is she? What time's she getting here?'

'Um, I think she's had another argument with her mum,' said Ben.

Tilly and Kya exchanged glances.

'She'd better come,' said Kya.

When Anna didn't turn up and didn't answer her phone, they agreed they had to go ahead and jump without her. The three of them walked the course together while Kya's mum and Ben's mum held onto their horses. Tilly's mum was working, and it felt strange to Tilly to be at a show without her usual supporters. The course was relatively straightforward and smaller than they would have to jump at the championships, but Angela had explained it would be better to go there feeling confident.

Tilly climbed up on to Magic not mentioning her worry about the combination to the others. It looked daunting: a vertical, one stride, then a parallel followed by two strides and another vertical.

'If you find a jump difficult, don't avoid it, practise it more.' She remembered Angela's words, and knew she was going to have to practise more and overcome her hang-up.

Magic took a bit of time getting rid of his enthusiasm, but he jumped well in the warm-up.

'Next to go: Tiger Lily Redbrow,' the steward shouted.

Tilly cantered into the ring, saluted to the judge, who promptly rang the bell, not giving her time to circle around the combination.

She and Magic were jumping a faultless round – she even felt relaxed and in a lovely rhythm approaching the dreaded combination. She sat quiet with her seat, kept her hands still, and jumped the first element well.

Then, out of nowhere a naughty Labrador came tearing into the ring, chasing after Magic, thinking it was a great game. Magic shot forward, flattening the next two elements of the combination. Somehow Tilly got him back under control to jump the last two fences while the distressed owner screamed loudly at her dog.

Tilly left the ring, trying to fight back the tears.

'Good job,' said Ben, as he entered the ring next.

'That was tough, but these things happen,' said Kya. She didn't sound sympathetic.

As Tilly got off and gave Magic a polo, how she wished her mum or Angela were there with her.

'Good boy, that wasn't your fault,' she said, trying to reassure Magic as well as herself.

She cheered up as she watched Ben and Hunter jump, making it all look very easy.

Kya and Bastion weren't so impressive. He was skittish on the way into the ring, despite Kya trying to settle him.

'Oh dear,' said Ben from the ringside. 'He's being a bit of a handful.'

'I'm sure she'll get him under control,' said Tilly, forgetting about her own problems as she watched Kya.

It was an awkward sight, especially after Kya had made such a point about her amazing bond with Bastion and how he would do anything for her. Once they got going they had a good round – messy over one of the doubles, but otherwise faultless.

They regrouped at Kya's lorry.

'Should we phone Anna again?' said Tilly. 'Make sure she's okay? It's such a shame she didn't jump.'

They all got on their phones. No reply from Anna. In the end, Kya decided to leave a message, but it wasn't a very friendly one.

'Anna? Where *are* you?' she snapped. 'We've been waiting and waiting. If you're not committed to the team, then you should say so, instead of wasting our time. Goodbye.'

'Whoa,' said Ben. 'Isn't that a bit harsh?'

Kya huffed.

'I'm in this to *win*,' she said. 'I don't want

my chances ruined by someone who can't be bothered to practise.'

Tilly winced. She wanted to win too, but she could see that the pressure was getting to Anna.

'I'm going to ring Anna's mum,' she said. 'Maybe she'll know what's going on.'

She got the number from Ben and tapped it into her phone. It rang. She felt nervous, knowing how stroppy Anna's mum could be.

'Hello?'

'Hi. This is Tilly from the Pony Club. We're wondering where Anna is? She's not turned up for the competition.'

Anna's mum heaved a sigh.

'Matinee is still in the field, Tilly. Anna refused to go to the competition altogether. Maybe you three can talk some sense into her? She won't talk to me at the moment.'

'We'll try,' said Tilly.

'*See*,' said Kya, when Tilly was off the phone. 'Anna's not committed. I told you. Maybe we should just replace her.'

Tilly said nothing. She knew it wasn't that

simple. They needed Anna's talent. And somehow, Anna needed convincing that she needed to compete.

After a busy and rather stressful day at the show, Tilly was glad to get Magic back to Silver Shoe Farm. She made sure she gave him a thorough groom. She checked his legs. Angela was always reminding everyone to get into the habit of feeling their horse's legs for any kind of heat or swelling, before and after work. She explained that if one leg was a lot hotter than another it could be an early warning sign that something was wrong.

'Oh, Magic,' Tilly said, as she gave him an apple. 'Let's just hope things work out better next weekend. If nothing else, you and I will try our best, won't we? And let's hope everyone has the sense to keep their dogs on a lead.'

Magic nickered and nuzzled her neck. She kissed his nose and stroked his shoulder.

Moments later, Angela came by. She had an armful of bridles.

'Good day?' she said. 'Feeling ready for the champs?'

Tilly frowned.

'Sort of.'

'What's up?'

'Team trouble,' said Tilly. 'I'm worried they're not going to pull together on the day.'

She was glad Angela had asked. Angela had years of experience as a top event rider, she was bound to know about team work. Tilly explained everything that had been going on.

'Sounds like *you* need to take the lead, Tilly,' said Angela. 'If your team mates have got issues, help them work them out. Do what it takes. Eventing is such a tough sport, a team needs to stick together. Support is the key. And as for the dog incident,' she added, 'don't waste time worrying about situations that are out of your control. Concentrate on thinking positively about the things you can control.'

Chapter Six

For the rest of the week, Tilly spent whatever spare time she had, before and after school, making sure that her team mates were competition-ready. She bought Ben an alarm clock, went through his kit with him, made sure his boots, hat, jodhpurs and jacket were clean and presentable, and gave him some ground-rules about when he could and couldn't use his phone (although she knew he wouldn't stick to them). She even helped him with Hunter.

'I'll do his plaits on competition morning if

you want,' she said. After all, Tilly was known for her perfect plaiting. She liked to divide the mane up equally into ten to twelve sections, making neat partings with a mane comb between each section of mane. Then she would meticulously plait and roll each section into a small ball. Angela had taught Tilly how to sew the plaits in with a needle and thread. Some people used small rubber bands but Tilly liked Angela's method best because it made the plaits more secure.

Then she made a plan to catch up with Anna. They arranged to meet at the park. Anna only lived a few streets away, so it was the ideal place. They sat on the swings near the fountain where the little kids splashed and played.

'So?' said Anna. 'What's with the park rendezvous? Normally we meet at the stables.'

'I thought it would be nice,' said Tilly. 'For a change. Listen. I know you're not sure about competing on Saturday. You're fed up of horses. You'd rather be doing gigs.'

Anna sighed and shrugged.

'I'm not fed up of horses, Tilly. I'm fed up of my mum. She won't leave me alone. She wants to live out her dream of being a top rider through me – but it's not what I want. I love Matinee. I enjoy hacking through forest trails on sunny days. I just don't want to compete. I don't want the pressure.'

'I get what you're saying,' said Tilly, 'but if you give it all up, don't you think you'd be wasting your talent? I mean, you've made the Pony Club championship team – doesn't that mean something?'

Anna shut her eyes and shook her head.

'Don't,' she said. 'Don't make me feel guiltier than I already do. You know Kya left a really nasty message on my phone?'

'I know,' said Tilly. 'I was there. She shouldn't have done that. I'm sorry.'

'It didn't help. I know you all want me to compete, but I don't need anyone's guilt trip. I already feel bad enough about letting Matinee down.'

'Matinee?'

'Well, you know, he loves competitions. He's that kind of horse. He wants to do his stuff, always eager.'

As she said this, an idea sparked in Tilly's head.

'In that case,' she said, looking Anna in the eye. 'Tell yourself you'll compete for him. Not for your mum. Not for Kya. Or Ben. Or me, for that matter. Do it for Matinee. Give him his chance to shine.'

Anna blinked. She looked up at the clouds, then at the grass, then back to Tilly.

'You know,' she said, slowly. 'I think you're right. That totally changes my perspective. That's it. I'm going to do it for Matinee. I'm going to give him the competition of his life. It's what he deserves.'

She threw her arms around Tilly and gave her a big hug. Tilly grinned, and felt a warm ripple of relief. Just in time!

After a week of running around after everyone else, Tilly hardly had time to get herself organised. She was in a bit of a panic because Angela had been away teaching for two days and was not getting back until late, so if Tilly wanted one more practice jumping through a combination, she would have to wait. She decided to do some flat work with Magic and have a last run through the test. She knew it was important to give him enough work so that he wasn't too fresh, but not so much that he would be tired and a little flat.

Afterwards she gave him a shampoo, using several buckets of luke-warm water. Magic always enjoyed this, except for having his head and ears washed when he would be uncooperative and stick his head as high as he could so that Tilly couldn't reach. Tilly grabbed the set of plastic steps.

'I can reach you now, cheeky,' she said, stretching up with a sponge. Magic playfully nudged her off the step.

'Okay, I get it, you want me to get as wet as you.'

'Who is giving who a bath?' asked Duncan, walking around the corner. 'When you've finished half-drowning each other, could you give me a hand turning some of the other horses out into the field?'

Angela was so lucky to have Duncan as head lad. He was always thorough and never left any of the horses standing in their stable all day without exercise. And just because Tilly had a major competition didn't mean she could ignore her usual Silver Shoe chores, other horses still needed turning out and feeding.

Having plaited and neatly trimmed Magic, Tilly cleaned her tack, checking the stitching on all the leather, then collected everything that she would need; numnahs, grooming kit, washing-down kit, boots, bandages, sweat rug, fly spray. It was a good job she had written a list in bed, the night before, otherwise she would never have remembered everything. All the gear was put neatly together in one pile and in another she put Magic's travel boots, rug and tail bandage ready for the morning.

'How are you getting on?' said Duncan, looking at his watch.

'I'm all done', replied Tilly. 'I'm just waiting for Angela to get back from teaching, so that I can give Magic a last pop through a combination.'

The phone rang. Angela had been held up in traffic and wasn't going to be home for another hour.

Tilly yawned. 'But I've got to practise the combination one more time.'

'You need sleep,' Duncan said. 'You won't do your best if you're exhausted.'

'I agree,' said Tilly's dad, stepping up behind them.

'Oh hi, Dad,' said Tilly.

'I've come to take you home, Tiger Lil'. I don't want you overdoing it before the big day.'

Tilly glanced over to the sand school then back at her dad's car in the drive. She had a horrible feeling about not getting enough practice in, but the thought of a comfy pillow was too tempting.

'I can't believe the day has finally arrived,' said her dad. 'After all these years, watching you trot, canter and gallop around that sand school, now you're heading for your first ever championships. I tell you, Tiger, I'm the proudest dad in the world.'

Tilly was up before dawn, awake with nerves, full of adrenalin. Despite her busy week, she was excited and feeling energetic. She jumped straight into the shower – five minutes of hot water, followed by a blast of cold as she'd read somewhere that cold showers pep up the body. She dressed and plaited her long brown hair. Her mum had organised breakfast and a packed lunch the night before. She did this every time Tilly competed. Tilly ate a bowl of muesli and two slices of toast, and downed a glass of orange juice.

Then it was time to get going: a quick drive to Silver Shoe Farm, feed and brush Magic, put his rugs, boots and bandages on, collect his tack, then load him into Kya's horsebox, alongside Bastion. Tilly's mum and dad were going to drive separately, bringing Mia and Tilly's younger brother, Adam. Angela and Duncan were also going – they didn't want to miss Tilly and Magic's performance at the championships.

Once Magic and Bastion were safely loaded, Tilly and Kya got into the front of the cab, alongside Kya's mum.

'See you there,' said Mia, hugging Tilly as she climbed into the cab.

'I wish you were coming in the lorry with us,' said Tilly.

'Sorry. There isn't room for extras,' said Kya, a little sniffily.

Mia just smiled and shrugged and waved them off, knowing full well there was plenty of room in the living area of the horsebox.

'Here goes,' said Tilly, her legs and arms quivering all of a sudden.

'First place here we come,' said Kya, with a cool smile.

'I like your confidence,' said Tilly. 'Look at me – I'm a bundle of nerves. How do you do it?'

'I'm always confident,' said Kya. 'It's the secret of my success.'

Tilly nodded and sat on her hands, trying to stop them shaking. She looked out of the window as the lorry pulled away from Silver Shoe and saw Mia and Angela and her mum and dad waving. Nerves or not, she knew she had their support. She was chuffed that so many people were going to watch her compete. It made her even more determined to do well.

The country estate was bustling with horseboxes, trailers, horses, riders and supporters. Every Pony Club event had a buzz about it, but this one was extra special. This was the one that counted. Once Kya's mum had managed to park, Tilly and Kya unloaded the horses and led them to the competitors' area. As Bastion stepped out he looked calm and composed. Magic meanwhile was full of beans. He kept tossing his head and pulling on his lead rope.

'Is he okay?' asked Kya. 'Are you having a problem keeping him under control?'

'Oh, no,' said Tilly. 'This is just Magic's way of getting psyched up. The excitement of a showground always gets him going.'

'It's just . . . you look like you're struggling. Bastion never gets like that. Maybe you need to use some of that "whispering" talent of yours?'

'He'll be fine,' said Tilly.

She smiled, but she couldn't help wondering if Kya's remark was intended as some kind of put-down. After all, she'd witnessed Kya struggle to gain Bastion's cooperation a couple of times, so there was no need for her to be smug. But no big deal. Perhaps it was her nerves talking. Maybe Kya was actually more jittery than she was letting on.

As they walked the horses into the competitors' area, Ben and Anna pulled in and parked in the space that had been saved next to Kya's lorry. Anna was chatting to her mum. To

Tilly's relief, they looked relaxed and happy, as though they were finally on each other's side. Ben unloaded Hunter. He was looking smarter than ever, organised and alert – *and* his phone was nowhere to be seen. Tilly was pleased. It seemed that her pep talk had worked. Hunter also looked good. His coat was shiny and his mane had been combed, ready for plaiting. Ben had obviously taken extra care.

'I hope you don't mind,' said Ben. 'I left the plaits for you, Tilly, like you said. Everyone goes on about how good you are at them.'

'No problem,' said Tilly. 'I'll do them now. And thanks for all the effort you've made. The judges are bound to be impressed.'

But as she began to part Hunter's mane, she noticed Kya watching her.

'Let's hope you compete as well as you plait,' said Kya, with a quick, tight smile.

Chapter Seven

The team filled out their registration forms and went through last-minute tack checks. The timings were such that all four of them were able to walk the cross country after their dressage. Tilly finished off plaiting Hunter, while Anna and Kya went to collect the programmes and numbers. Ben offered water to the horses before taking their travelling boots and bandages off. As they worked, they couldn't avoid catching snippets of competition gossip.

'Someone in the toilets said that the cross country is tougher than ever,' said Anna.

'Apparently there are some monster ditches.'

Tilly winced and tried not to worry. She was planning to walk the course after her dressage test, which would allow her to size up the challenges and work out what line to take.

'Well,' said Kya, '*I* heard a rumour that the British selectors are here.'

At this, Tilly's ears pricked.

'Seriously?'

'They're looking for riders to join their training programme.'

Now the butterflies really kicked in. Winning the championships would be one thing, but being selected for the Junior Squad? Tilly folded her arms, unfolded them, chewed her thumb then stopped chewing. She didn't know what to do with herself. The excitement was hard to contain. Then, just as things couldn't get any better, a familiar face walked past.

'It's Harry Grey,' whispered Anna, pretending to swoon. 'Handsome Harry.'

Harry Grey was one of the region's most promising young male riders, with his liver chestnut gelding, Nobleman. He trained with a rival pony club, Marsh Union Hunt, on the other side of the county. Tilly had seen him at competitions, so it was no surprise that he was at the championships. She checked the programme and saw he was on a very strong team, good enough to scoop first place.

'Less of the "handsome",' said Ben. 'Let's not forget Harry Grey is the enemy.'

Anna giggled.

'I'm going to make it my mission to spend at least five minutes talking to him today. He's so fit. What do you reckon, Kya?'

Kya shrugged.

'I've known Harry since I was a baby,' she said dismissively. 'Our dads used to work together.'

Tilly rolled her eyes. Of course, Kya *would* know the most attractive boy in the whole of the Pony Club. It was starting to seem as if she always had to do better than anyone else. As Harry walked by he waved, but it wasn't clear who he was waving at. Kya? Anna? Both of them?

Then he spoke.

'Good luck, guys,' he said. 'But not too much good luck, hey? Rival teams and all.'

Then he smiled at Tilly.

'Especially you. I hear *you're* the secret weapon.'

'Me?'

'The word going round is that you and Magic Spirit have really come on. I'll be looking out.'

Tilly grinned. She never had much time for boy-talk – but for Harry she'd make an exception.

'Thanks,' she said.

With the prospect of the junior selectors, not to mention Harry Grey, on her mind, Tilly got ready for her dressage test. She buttoned her jacket, smoothed her plaits, adjusted her riding hat, ran through the dressage test in her head, then gave her boots a last-minute polish. As soon as she mounted, she could feel Magic's eagerness.

'Ben, you couldn't just put some fly spray on Magic could you, please?' asked Tilly as Magic fidgeted impatiently. 'Steady there, boy,' she whispered. 'Calm down. Calm down. Let's be chilled and relaxed.'

They walked quietly to the dressage warm-up area. Tilly had given herself forty minutes to get ready for her test. She knew she had to get the timing right. She had learned from past competitions that Magic easily got lazy to the leg if she gave him too long and lost a bit of the wow factor, too little and he had all the wow factor plus a few cheeky bucks and squeals! Angela warned her not to ask too much from him in the warm-up. *'You want to save his best work for the test.'*

The steward came to let Tilly know she was next to go.

'Remember Magic needs his boots taking off, you don't want to get eliminated,' Kya warned. She'd learned the hard way after she had been eliminated at a previous competition for leaving a pair of Bastion's exercise boots on.

'Oh, thanks for reminding me,' said Tilly, glad that Kya seemed to be back onside again.

Anna walked over and took Magic's boots off, Ben sprayed more fly spray and Kya sponged the white froth that had collected around Magic's mouth. 'This is what being in a team is all about,' thought Tilly. 'Everyone being hands on and helping.'

'Good luck, girl,' said Ben as she trotted off towards the arena.

'Good luck,' cried Anna.

'Show them what you're both made of,' Kya said, genuinely.

Tilly suddenly felt very nervous. She had never performed in front of so many people. Even though her parents, Angela, Duncan and Mia were all there, along with Penny and her team mates supporting her, she felt a new kind of pressure. The feeling that she didn't want to let her team down.

Tilly reminded herself that she had to give a good first impression as she trotted to the outside of the dressage arena. A rather fierce-looking judge wearing a bowler hat sat at C at the far end of the centre line. He rang his bell for Tilly to start. As soon as she heard it, Tilly tensed up and immediately felt Magic tighten beneath her.

'Remember to breathe,' she told herself, as she turned to enter through the white boards. Magic quickly relaxed as the tension left Tilly.

She dropped her shoulders and back, stretched up taller and rode positively down the centre line. Magic grew two inches and she sensed he really wanted to show himself off as they rode their fifteen-metre circle. Tilly gave and retook the inside rein on the first half of the circle. Magic never altered his outline. She rode a very accurate three-loop serpentine before executing a beautiful transition to canter. All Magic's canter work was very balanced and the transitions up and down were so smooth. He really stretched his neck out in the free walk on a long rein, proving to the judge how relaxed he was. Tilly, concentrating on every step of the way, quietly shortened her reins.

'Good boy,' she thought to herself, as Magic didn't even seem to think of anticipating what came next. It was the first time he had managed the whole walk movement without jogging. They repeated the exercise as faultlessly on the other rein. Just the medium trot to go. Tilly turned a very balanced corner, sat a little deeper and barely asked Magic to extend his stride. His hind legs came more underneath him as his front legs reached further out ahead. Everyone watching gasped at his majestic splendour.

'Concentrate, Tilly, concentrate, we're nearly there,' she thought as she made her final turn onto the centre line. Just at the vital moment, sensing Magic about to swing his bottom to the right, she put her right leg on, stopping him from doing it and made the transition to halt. She waited a couple of seconds, showing the judge how well Magic could establish his halt, before saluting by dropping her right hand to her side and nodding her head.

Tilly beamed from ear to ear, and couldn't

stop patting Magic as he walked out of the arena.

'Perfect,' said Angela, releasing her fingers which had been crossed the whole way through Tilly's test. 'Definitely a personal best.'

The others were all cheering and clapping.

Tilly wanted to whoop for joy, but she managed to keep it together until her score was announced.

'We have a new early leader,' the commentator said. 'Tiger Lily Redbrow riding Magic Spirit has a penalty score of twenty-eight.'

Top marks!

She couldn't believe it. She knew the test had gone well, but she never liked to assume. Everyone congratulated her on hearing the result.

'Well done, boy!' she said, patting Magic's shoulder again as she rode him back to the lorry. 'Clever, clever boy!'

Duncan helped her wash Magic down, then offered to look after him while she went to watch her team-mates in action. Next up were Kya and Bastion. Tilly wasn't surprised, but she was very pleased, that they also performed a super test. Kya looked very stylish in her new made-to-measure riding jacket. Her test was as polished as her new black boots. Tilly couldn't quite believe all the new gear. Ben and Hunter did well too. They dropped points for a clumsy stumble, but still got a good score.

'It's going well,' said Angela, squeezing Tilly's arm. 'Your dressage was a pleasure to watch. Just what the judges like to see. Keep this up and you'll be in with a chance.'

'I hope so. Have you heard any of the rumours about junior selectors?'

'I've seen a few keen-eyed people about,' said Angela, smiling. 'I recognised one of them from the eventing circuit. He's over there. His name's John Pickford.'

She pointed to a man wearing a red polo shirt and sunglasses.

'Don't worry, Tilly, he's bound to notice you. But remember, it's not just your riding he'll be looking at. It's the whole package – how you present yourself, how you care for your horse, how you work with your team mates. It's not just skill that will get you noticed, but attitude too.'

The last pair to perform their dressage test was Anna and Matinee. Having watched them struggle in the practice session at Silver Shoe, Tilly felt a bit anxious. But as soon as they walked into the arena and gave the judges a confident salute, she knew she had nothing to worry about. They performed brilliantly. For the duration of the test, Anna had a look of determined focus. Clearly, she'd taken on board Tilly's advice and had committed herself to giving Matinee the best ride she could.

Between dressage and cross country, the team had time to get a drink and a quick snack.

'I'm starving,' said Ben. 'Competing always makes me ravenous.'

He ripped into a family bag of crisps and stared munching.

'You won't get much fuel from crisps,' said Kya. 'You're an athlete, you know. You should eat more healthily.'

Ben just shrugged.

'Whatever.'

Tilly looked at her watch.

'We've got an hour before we have to get ready. We'd better crack on and walk the cross country. See what this "scary" course is all about.'

'Good idea,' said Kya.

The four of them made their way over to the start of the cross country course, joined by Angela and her invaluable advice, and Scruff, the Redbrows' beloved Jack Russell terrier, who was jumping up and down excitedly, playing with his lead. The course consisted of twenty numbered fences set out on a gently undulating track. It was by far the biggest track that Tilly had ever jumped.

The first three fences were widely spaced and not too difficult.

'Don't be complacent early on, it's important to get a good positive rhythm,' Angela advised.

The fourth fence was a long drop into a wooded copse, followed by a sharp right-hand turn out and over a ditch, followed in one stride by an angled rail.

'Keep your legs on here, but not too quick, the horses have got to have a chance to see where they're going, and make sure you sit back a little over the drop.' Angela walked confidently on, not noticing the nervous looks from behind.

Then the course went uphill with a couple more straightforward fences, before they got to a tricky combination, which involved jumping a right-handed corner fence followed three strides later by a left-handed corner. Angela showed them the correct line to approach on and they all walked the distance between each fence. Anna went pale knowing that Matinee's stride wasn't as long as the other horses'.

'Just send him forward a bit more, once you've landed after the first corner,' Angela said.

'You'll be fine,' said Tilly encouragingly.

'Whatever happens stay glued to your line,' warned Angela as she marched to the next fence.

They walked down a slight incline and came to three steps leading down.

'Again not too fast here, I think you should nearly bring them back to a trot just before the top step, and watch you don't get in front of them.' Tilly knew exactly what Angela meant because she often used to go forward too early with her upper body, and get tipped off balance.

'It will help if you stick your legs forward as you go down the steps,' Angela added.

As they approached the barrels before the water, Tilly lost concentration.

'Hi, guys,' said a voice.

It was Harry Grey and one of his Marsh Union Hunt team mates.

'Well done in the dressage,' he said. 'I see the North Cosford crew got the best scores of the day.'

'Didn't do too badly yourself,' said Ben, through gritted teeth.

Tilly sensed their rivalry – and it wasn't just about dressage. It was boys' stuff, a top-dog popularity competition. Ben crossed his arms. Anna giggled. Tilly smiled. Then Kya stepped forward, smoothed her hair, and gave Harry a hug.

'Hi, babes,' she said. 'How *are* you?'

'Oh, hi, Kya,' said Harry, flustered. 'So it's true you've moved back to the area? Still into eventing, then?'

'Of course I am.'

'And your horse?'

'Bastion? He's going from strength to strength.'

'Great.'

'It's our bond,' she said. 'Everyone's been talking about it. As long as he's my horse and I'm his rider, nothing can stop us.'

Tilly gasped – that was exactly what people always said about her and Magic. Once again she got the feeling that Kya was trying to outdo her. Perhaps this was the side of her that Ben and Anna had warned her about? Annoyed, she stepped forward, and gave Harry a smile. Harry smiled back.

'Hi, Tilly,' he said.

'Hi. How's Nobleman doing?' she said. 'Do you think he'll enjoy this course? I saw him earlier. He's quite a size. Is he easy to handle?'

'Oh, yeah, he's a dream. Looks like a beast, but honestly, he doesn't ride as big as he looks. Try riding him sometime, you'll see what I mean.'

'I'd love to.'

She glanced round to see Kya glaring, eyes blazing with envy. Harry seemed not to notice.

'And maybe you'll let me ride Magic Spirit,' he said. 'I was watching him in the dressage. He's so light on his feet, yet I bet he's got loads of power?'

'Definitely,' said Tilly. 'You'll see it in the show-jumping. He jumps like a stag. And I can't wait to get him out on this cross country. He's brave, but sometimes gets a little strong.'

'An all-rounder, eh? Horses like that are so special. Where did you find him?'

'Um . . .'

Tilly shuffled uneasily, and started twiddling her horsehair bracelets.

'We kind of found each other,' she said, hoping that would satisfy Harry's interest.

She didn't want the story of how she didn't officially own Magic Spirit to become the talk of the championships. She didn't want to be judged by the fact that Magic had been a rescue horse, or that unlike Kya, she hadn't been riding since she was three. And she certainly didn't want the matter to go public. Now that Magic was clearly worth something, the more people knew about his story, the more likelihood there was that someone would come out of the woodwork and claim him for their own.

'Let's carry on walking, shall we?' she said, quickly changing the subject. 'Otherwise we won't get to see the rest of the course.'

'Good idea,' said Harry. 'By the way, I'm glad to hear you and Magic are good at show jumping.

I've heard that the last obstacle is a particularly tricky combination.'

Tilly gulped.

'Really?'

'I hate those, don't you? I knew they would build it up to height though. They do it every year. I spent most of last week practising.'

'Wise move,' said Tilly quietly, wishing that she had practised a combination for one last time. Then she remembered that it wasn't just riding skill that the selectors looked out for, but all-round attitude.

She only hoped Angela had been right about that.

Chapter Eight

With the prospect of the show jumping round ahead, Tilly did her best to put aside her worries and focus on the cross country. Apart from the trebles in the show jumping, Magic loved all kinds of jumps and the range of ditches and logs on the course looked exciting. A penalty-free round would allow them to keep their lead, or at least give them a chance.

While she waited for her turn to start, she had a sneaky peek at Harry and Nobleman. Harry had been right. Despite his size, he was very light on his feet. He galloped away from the start really meaning business and, according to the commentator, completed a practically perfect round with only one time penalty. Tilly clapped and cheered, despite disapproving looks from Ben.

'You can't encourage Harry Grey,' he complained. 'He's the enemy.'

Tilly's cheeks went pink. Ben shook his head.

'Oh, boy. Not you too. Just my luck that my number-one rival is fancied by the rest of my team.'

'I don't . . . I just . . . it's not . . . I just think Harry's a good rider, that's all.'

Ben shook his head.

'And the rest.'

Suddenly, Tilly heard her name over the loud-speaker, requesting her to head for the starting box.

'That's your call,' said Ben. 'Good luck. Kick on! Go for it!'

Tilly smiled.

'Thanks. You too.'

By the time they entered the starting box,

Magic was dancing on his toes, itching to get going. Keenness was always a good sign. It tended to mean he was full of bounce and energy. Tilly twiddled her horsehair bracelets.

'Do me proud, boy,' she whispered, knowing that if there was a chance she could mess up the show jumping, she had to prove herself on the cross country. She didn't even have to ask him to go, as soon as the countdown finished, off they went.

The ground was springy underfoot, not too hard, but not too soft either. Magic galloped to the first fence. Tilly crouched low, her gaze fixed forwards. She felt balanced and light as he flew along ready for anything. More than that, she felt happy. She and Magic were doing what they loved best.

They cleared the first few jumps easily, the log drop, corners, steps down. They were on top form. They cranked up the pace on the uphill. The course was lined with spectators, but to Tilly they were mere streaks of colour that she barely noticed as she galloped on. The barrels lay ahead, the murky water on the other side.

'Come on, boy!' cried Tilly. 'We love water!'

Magic leapt the barrels, up and over with his front legs, his hind legs tucked neatly under him. Tilly leaned back as they landed and splashed their way through the water. A couple of ditches, another flat stretch, then finally, the home stretch consisting of an awkward turn round a tree to a narrow arrowhead and then the last two fences.

They stepped up the pace even more for the finishing straight, a full-on gallop across the flat. And as they came through the finish flags, Tilly didn't even need to look to know that she'd made the time. Not a single penalty. She'd managed to pull off the ride of her life.

It was only when she dismounted that she became aware of the chatter. As she started to lead Magic back towards Kya's lorry, she heard whispering. She heard her name! Two girls she didn't recognise were pointing at Magic.

'I heard that horse isn't hers,' said one of the

girls, loud enough for Tilly to hear. 'Apparently he was stolen. Doesn't even belong to her.'

'Yeah, that's what I heard too,' said the other. 'It's so unfair. I mean, we've looked after our horses all our lives, then Tiger Lily Redbrow comes along, steals a horse, and reckons she can win everything. It's like cheating.'

Tilly's heart lurched. It didn't matter that she didn't know them, or that they were obviously just a pair of Pony Club mean-girls – the story had come out. Somehow, Tilly and Magic's secret had escaped. She looked around in a panic and realised these girls weren't the only ones talking. It felt like everyone was staring, whispering, pointing. She felt sick. She clung to Magic, did her best to look ahead, to lead him through the crowd.

How?

How did the story get out?

But, of course, Tilly knew. There was only one person on the team who knew her secret, one person who seemed to have it in for her. She looked back across the sea of faces and horses and saw Kya hanging from Harry Grey's shoulder, looking very pleased with herself. Tilly felt overwhelmed with anger. She'd been betrayed. She marched a puffing Magic over towards Kya.

'Oh hi, Tilly,' said Kya. 'Sorry, can't chat. Just about to compete.'

'How *dare* you?' said Tilly, unable to contain herself.

'I'm sorry. Like, what is *this* all about?'

'You told everyone, didn't you? What I'd asked you to keep secret, you spread around. Now everyone's talking and gossiping about me–'

'I've got no idea what she's talking about,' Kya snapped, keeping hold of Harry.

'Yeah, you do,' said Harry, as he glanced from Kya to Tilly. 'You were saying just now, about Tilly being an orphan and Magic being stolen . . .'

Kya's perfect skin flushed red. Tilly glared at her.

'How could you?'

'I – I didn't realise it was private information,' she said. 'Sorry.'

'Yes, you did!' said Tilly, almost shaking with fury. 'Of course, you did! They warned me about you. Ben and Anna warned me, but I didn't believe them. I gave you a chance. How wrong was I? Anyway, I never stole Magic. I rescued him. *Rescued*. There's a difference.'

'Yes, whatever,' said Kya.

She sniffed and pushed past Tilly.

'Excuse me. Time I got on for the cross country.'

And with that, she swept off, leaving Tilly feeling shaky and upset. Harry tried to put a comforting arm around her, but it didn't help. All she wanted was Magic. She hugged him tightly. She didn't want to watch Kya's round. She didn't care anymore.

Tilly took Magic back to the lorry and washed him down, but she was still so angry, she wasn't as gentle as usual. Magic stamped his hoof.

'Sorry, boy,' she said. 'But it's not fair. Why is she being so mean? What have I ever done to her?'

Fifteen minutes went by, Ben and Anna came over, with Kya trailing behind. Kya looked as if she'd been crying. Ben and Anna looked cross.

'Tilly,' said Ben. 'What's going on? Why were you arguing with Kya just before her cross country?'

Tilly blinked.

'She was spreading rumours about me,' she said, defensively.

'Well, thanks to your outburst,' said Ben, 'we've lost our chance to win.'

'*What*?'

'Kya was so upset about you having a go at her,' said Anna, 'she totally messed up.'

'Two run-outs,' Kya sniffed. 'It was the worst ride of my life!'

She burst into tears. Tilly didn't know what to say.

'But, I . . . she . . . I didn't mean . . .'

Ben just scowled.

'Great timing, Tilly. Good one.'

Chapter Nine

Magic flared his nostrils and swung his quarters round. It was obvious he didn't like hearing the tense voices around him. Tilly stroked his nose, but it didn't help.

'He doesn't like arguments,' Anna observed.

'No one likes arguments,' said Tilly.

Least of all her. She wanted to explain why she'd had a go at Kya, that Kya had started it, that Kya had been malicious, but, at the same time, she knew she had to face up to the situation. She knew she was as responsible as anyone for Kya's cross country catastrophe. She realised she'd picked the wrong moment to confront her and now she felt sick with guilt.

'I'm sorry, guys,' she said, staring at the ground. 'I don't know what to say.'

'You can start by making up,' said Ben. 'Sort out your differences before you jeopardise the show jumping as well.'

He and Anna stormed off, leaving Tilly and Kya standing there with Magic between them, swishing his tail. The silence was horrible. All Tilly wanted to do was jump on Magic's back and gallop away. Just as she was just about to apologise, Kya interrupted.

'That was *so* selfish, you know?' she hissed. 'You made a total fool of me.'

Suddenly Tilly's urge to say sorry evaporated.

'What about what you did to *me*?' said Tilly. 'I told you my story in private, not so you could broadcast it around the Pony Club.'

'What's the big deal? So I told a few people. Who *cares*? It doesn't justify you ruining my cross country. Do you have any idea how that felt? We might not win, thanks to you.'

Tilly's anger boiled. She felt the muscles in her arms and legs tense.

'You can't blame it all on me!' she yelled. 'So don't try to.'

'Who *are* you anyway?' said Kya. 'You and your magic horse and your stupid plaits and your "Look at me I'm Silver Shoe's best horse whisperer" rubbish. I don't buy it.'

She grabbed Tilly's arm.

'And what's with the horsehair bracelets?'

Fuming, Tilly yanked her hand away, but as she did, one of her bracelets – the oldest one, given to her by her mum just before she'd died – caught on Kya's thumb. It came apart, fell and landed in the dirt. Tilly gasped.

'My bracelet!'

She dropped to the ground and scooped it up, but emotion overwhelmed her. Her eyes filled with tears and she started to sob. Kya, realising she'd gone too far, stepped forward and put her hand on Tilly's shoulder.

'I – I'm sorry, Tilly. I didn't mean to . . .'

But it was too late. The damage had been

done. Tilly's horsehair bracelets were her most treasured possessions. Kya had insulted her in the worst way possible. She reattached it round her wrist and ran from the scene, tears streaming down her face. But as she ran she bumped headlong into a man who'd been standing nearby. She looked up, muttered an apology. Their eyes met, then she realised it was John Pickford, the man in the red T-shirt that Angela had pointed out earlier. The junior selector. He'd seen everything.

Angela's advice kept revolving round Tilly's head: *It's not just skill they're looking for, but attitude, team work*. She and Kya had hardly presented a good example. And now she had the show jumping coming up and the dreaded combination fence.

She wiped her tears and breathed out her stress. When she felt calmer, she returned to Magic.

'Oh, boy! What a disaster!'

Magic lowered his head. Tilly rested her cheek against his nose.

'At least you understand me,' she whispered, as he pricked his ears and whickered.

They watched the first few competitors return from the show jumping arena. The horses looked hot and tired and the riders looked drained.

'What a course!' said one of them.

'That was really difficult. I messed it up completely,' said another.

It didn't sound too encouraging. Tilly did her best to distract herself by checking Magic's tack. She made sure everything was adjusted correctly, that there was no dirt or grit beneath the saddle and straps. She tried to put the argument with Kya out of her head and get into competition mode, but she couldn't escape the prospect of the combination fence. Her championship dreams seemed as if they were falling apart. Desperate to hear a friendly voice, she found a quiet spot under a tree and called Brook.

'Tilly? How's it going? Aren't you at the

champs today? I've been thinking of you.'

'Oh, Brook, it's all gone wrong,' she sniffed.

'What? What's the matter?'

Tilly recounted everything, from her worries about Magic being taken from her, to Kya's jealous comments, to their awful argument which had been witnessed by the junior selector.

'What can I do?' said Tilly. 'Kya's supposed to be my team mate, but at the moment she hates me. I've worked so hard to get here and now it's all hopeless.'

Brook sighed.

'I know, Tilly. You deserve it more than anyone. So does Magic. All I can say is stay true to who you are. Don't let the rumours get you down. Sometimes competition brings out the worst in people. Jealousy can have a huge effect on people. It happens everywhere, you mustn't let it distract you. No matter how hard that seems. I've seen all sorts of drama going on behind the scenes, but the best riders rise above it. They don't get distracted from their goal.'

Tilly sniffed, wiped her eyes.

'Thanks,' she said.

'I'm always here for you, Tilly, any time. One day, we'll be travelling the eventing circuit together with our big lorry and string of top horses.'

Tilly laughed.

'Believe in yourself,' said Brook. 'And believe in Magic.'

Just as she'd hoped, Brook's words gave Tilly the drive she needed to face the show jumping. She returned from walking the course, mounted Magic and went to the collecting ring, where she warmed up and popped him over some jumps. Usually, at this point in a competition, he was totally psyched, fired up and ambitious to do his best. But something had changed. All of a sudden he felt stone-heavy. Tilly felt bad – obviously the stress had got to him too. One of the stewards looked down at his clipboard and gave Tilly a nod.

'Tiger Lily Redbrow and Magic Spirit. You're next.'

Tilly pushed her heels in the stirrups and nudged Magic forward. She tried to focus, to encourage him forward, but she felt weak with nerves. Her fear of the combination fence, the thought of coming so far and throwing the competition away at the final obstacle was all too much. It was filling her head with negative thoughts. As she reached the arena, she heard a shout behind her. It was Kya.

'Oh, no. What does *she* want?' Tilly whispered.

Magic gave a snort.

'Wait,' said Kya. 'I've got a tip for that difficult treble combination – I meant to tell you before, but . . . well . . . Anyway, I overheard one of the course designers talking about how to tackle it. He said the secret is to establish an energetic, forward canter – not too fast, but lots of power. Use more leg and keep a steady rein contact. Then keep that leg on over the first element, but don't overchase to the second element, so you can give your horse time to jump out.'

Tilly blinked and nodded.

'Go for it,' said Kya. 'I bet you'll do brilliantly.'

Tilly could see that she meant it. Suddenly, all the negative thoughts were replaced by a positive plan. The two girls smiled at each other.

'Team work,' said Tilly.

'Too right,' said Kya. 'No more arguments.'

Tilly sat up in the saddle and squeezed with her legs. Magic moved forward confidently. It was as if he'd got his enthusiasm back, now that Tilly was happy again.

Chapter Ten

Tilly walked Magic into the arena, and surveyed the arrangement of doubles, oxers and triple bars. Nothing she hadn't jumped before.

'Think about a good rhythm. Sit still. Keep your eyes up.' She cantered up to the treble, stopping approach in her head. The bell rang. She saluted the judges, reined back, quickly touched her lucky horsehair bracelets and picked up an energetic canter.

The first fence was easy – a simple ascending narrow oxer, something she had cleared a million times before, followed six strides later by a tall vertical. Fences three and four were trickier, off a left-handed turn there was a wide oxer followed by a double made up of two vertical rails three strides later. Magic knew exactly what he was supposed to do. Tilly barely needed to ask. They were so deep in concentration that they didn't notice the crowd or the unfamiliar surroundings. Except for one tiny rub on the planks, Magic cleared the next eight fences with ease.

But then came the final line. Thirteen A, B and C. The treble combination. 'Unlucky for some,' she thought, 'but not for me!'

Tilly gulped back her nerves and turned onto her line. All she could see was a mass of yellow and green. It was hard on the approach to assess, all three elements seemed to blur into one. She had Magic in a balanced, powerful canter, not too quick – just as Kya had suggested. She sat quiet with her seat. Moments later the first element was upon them. They met it spot on, resulting in a good clean jump. One down, two to go. Tilly immediately squeezed with her leg, but sat as still as she could with her seat and upper body, not giving Magic any excuse to rush forward. He flew over the B element, trying his hardest, leaving so much room between his hooves and the top pole that he jumped it too well which made his stride to C very short, and his last jump awkward. Tilly's heart sank as she heard the rattle of the pole.

Confused by all the clapping and cheering, she glanced back at the final element. To her delight it was still standing. Although Magic had hit it, the pole had not fallen.

As her hand flew to her mouth in surprise, she glimpsed her lucky bracelet and felt pure joy radiate inside her.

'Well done, boy,' she cried, patting Magic's neck. 'You star. Good boy.'

She saw her parents grinning and waving, then she caught Harry Grey's eye. He gave her a thumbs up. She was so thrilled she didn't know whether to laugh or cry.

'Wow, Magic! You're a star. You're going to get the biggest bag of carrots ever!'

She leaned forward, throwing both arms around his neck. As she did, he turned his head, almost as if he was trying to give her a kiss back.

As Tilly dismounted, Anna, Ben and Kya ran towards her.

'Brilliantly ridden! Amazing! Well done!'

They jumped up and down in a group hug, the arguments forgotten. Tilly took the opportunity to squeeze Kya's arm.

'Thanks,' she said. 'Your advice about that combination made all the difference.'

Then, over Kya's shoulder, she caught a glimpse of John Pickford. Once again, he was watching. She didn't say anything to the others. She simply hoped he was noting the positive feeling.

'Do you think we've done enough to win?' said Anna. 'I mean, despite our mess up in the cross country, our dressage was top and we've all had good show jumping rounds.'

Ben shook his head.

'It'll be close,' he said. 'I guess it depends how

Handsome Harry and his crew perform in the show jumping. Let's go and watch them.'

Harry and his team, as predicted, did well. Harry in particular delivered a classy clear, but others in his team all had one fence down each. They weren't as good as North Cosford, but it all came down to the lowest overall penalty across the three disciplines. Tilly knew it was going to be close. They'd beaten Marsh Union Hunt in the dressage and jumping, but the cross country fiasco had let them down.

They gathered by the judge's enclosure and waited for the scores. Kya paced. Anna chewed her nails. Ben was on the phone to his girlfriend (they seemed to have made up, which meant he was on the phone more than ever) and Tilly twiddled her horsehair bracelets. The wait was unbearable. All the effort she and Magic had put in over the last few years seemed to have been channelled into this moment.

One of the judges raised his hand and tapped his microphone. The crowds stopped and listened.

'And so to announce, in reverse order, the winners of this year's Open Pony Club Team Event Championships. In third place, with one hundred and sixty-five points, the Crannock Chase Branch–'

A cheer erupted from the crowd.

'And in second place, with one hundred and forty-eight penalty points . . .'

Tilly held her breath.

'The North Cosford Branch.'

'YEAH!'

'That's us!' said Anna.

The crowd cheered. Tilly looked at her team mates. She didn't know whether to be pleased or disappointed. She knew it was an achievement. Second place was nothing to be ashamed of, especially out of so many teams. But it wasn't first place. First place went to Harry and co.

Tilly did her best to hide her disappointment

and congratulated Harry and the rest of the Marsh Union Hunt Team on their victory. Despite all their rivalry, Ben and Anna did too. They seemed comfortable with second. Even Kya had a smile on her face.

'To be honest,' she said, 'after my cross country abomination, I thought I'd knocked us right down the ranks. Second place is proof that even when things go wrong, we're still the most talented riders out there. If we hadn't messed up, we'd have definitely won.'

'Next time,' said Anna.

'As long as there's no more arguing,' said Ben.

Tilly looked at her feet, felt the responsibility on her shoulders. Even though everyone was taking it well, she still felt guilty. They'd so nearly won. If she hadn't had a go at Kya just before her cross country, would the final result have been different? While everyone laughed and celebrated around them, that thought weighed her down.

Harry's mum, a large, smiley lady with blue

eyes, came forward holding a huge strawberry gateau.

'I told Harry that if he and Nobleman won, I'd bring his favourite cake for him. Here we go. Who wants a slice? There's plenty for everyone.'

As they tucked into the cake, Tilly held back. She was pleased for Harry, of course she was. Of all people, she was glad it was him at the top. She had watched him carefully and liked the way he rode. She liked him – a lot. But she felt as if she had let her team down, after all she'd done too. It was hard to bear.

Harry offered her a slice of his cake.

'Looks delicious,' she said. 'But no thanks. I – I'm not really that hungry.'

To make matters worse, from the corner of her eye, she could see two of the junior selectors, John Pickford and a young woman, talking to Harry's riding instructor. Then they came over to Harry.

'Congratulations on Marsh Union Hunt's win,' said the woman. 'We're impressed with what we've seen. We're looking for new talent to take forward for the Junior Squad. It's a big step. We only take on riders who are absolutely committed, but we've had our eye on you. Would you be interested?'

Harry's eyes bulged. He nearly choked on his cake.

'Are you kidding? I'd love it!'

He beamed and thanked the selectors.

To Tilly, it was like a cannon ball thudding into her. She was about to turn and walk away, when John beckoned her.

'We've been watching your team too, Tiger Lily.'

Tilly swallowed, closed her eyes, and dreaded what he was going to say next – the argument, the shouting in front of the horses, the emotional drama.

'We appreciate the pressure that this level of competition can place on our young riders. We observed that your team had some issues, but what really caught our attention was how you were able to put aside your differences when the crunch came. That takes great strength of character. Combined with the obvious talent the four of you have, we feel we'd like to take the North Cosford Team forward too.'

Tilly's mouth opened in a big O. Kya and Ben and Anna glanced at each other.

'You mean we've made the training squad? We're in?'

The selectors nodded.

'Congratulations everyone and, of course, well done to your brilliant horses. Without them none of you would be here, so make sure they get rewarded for their hard work. You'll each receive a letter formally outlining the opportunity we are offering you, so look out for it in the post, and obviously we'll need to discuss training requirements with your parents. Junior Squad is a big commitment and it has to fit in with school work, but we like to think that among the eight of you to join our existing squad, we have the future of British eventing talent.'

Everyone applauded. Tilly grinned from ear to ear. She caught Harry's eye.

'I'll have a bit of that cake now, please,' she said.

The Junior Squad letter arrived two days later. Tilly was sitting at the breakfast table with Adam and her parents on either side.

'What's it say? What's it say?' asked Adam, eagerly.

Tilly scanned the words. When she got halfway through she shrieked.

'It says our first training will be a week-long camp at the stables of international event rider Livvy James!'

'I've heard of her!' said Tilly's mum.

'Of course you have,' said Tilly. 'I've got posters of her all over my walls. She's one of my idols. She's competed all over the world. She's ridden some of the most amazing horses ever. I can't believe it! We're going to spend a week at her stables!'

She grinned, clutching the letter to her chest.

'I must tell Brook . . . and Angela . . . and Mia . . . and Duncan . . . and . . .'

'And Magic,' said Tilly's dad, reading her mind. 'He'll be going training with you. Come on. I'll give you a lift to Silver Shoe, so you can break the good news to him.'

Tilly scooted out of her chair, grabbed her boots and a bumper bag of carrots that she'd bought from the farm shop.

Magic was in the long field with a few of his Silver Shoe friends, Angela's sleek eventer, Pride and Joy and mischievous Buttons, the grey pony, and, of course, his best friend, Thumbelina, the shaggy little Shetland who had helped him conquer his fear of other horses. They were enjoying the early morning sun, running up and down the fence-line, then rolling on the grass like playful children. Magic, in particular, looked contented and full of life. It didn't matter how many times she looked at him, groomed him, exercised him, jumped him – he always amazed her. She knew she'd never forget the malnourished, frightened horse he'd once been. But every day that horrible time seemed further and further away.

As soon as Magic saw Tilly, he pricked his ears and galloped to the fence. She held out her arms, stroked his mane, and then fed him a carrot.

'Fancy a week with Livvy James?' she said. 'Junior Squad Training starts soon!'

Magic just crunched his treat, and then sniffed at her pocket for more.

'Trust me,' she said. 'I think you'll enjoy it.'

She paused, looking out over the field, across the fresh green grass, gazing into the distance.

'As long as you and I are together, Magic, as long as we're a team, I think our dreams will keep coming true, don't you?'

Magic lifted his head and gave a happy whinny.

Pippa Funnell

"Winning is amazing for a minute, but then I am striving again to reach my next goal."

I began learning to ride when I was six, on a little pony called Pepsi.

When I was seven, I joined my local Pony Club – the perfect place to learn more about riding and caring for horses.

By the time I was fourteen and riding my first horse, Sir Barnaby, my dream of being an event rider was starting to take shape.

Two years later, I was offered the opportunity to train as a working pupil in Norfolk with Ruth McMullen, the legendary riding teacher. I jumped at the chance.

In 1987, Sir Barnaby and I won the individual gold together at the Young Rider European Championships, which was held in Poland.

Since then, hard work and determination have taken me all the way to the biggest eventing competitions in the world. I've been lucky and had success at major events like Bramham, Burghley, Badminton, Luhmühlen, Le Lion d'Angers, Hickstead, Blenheim, Windsor, Saumur, Pau, Kentucky – and the list goes on . . .

I married William Funnell in 1993. William is an international show jumper and horse breeder. He has helped me enormously with my show jumping. We live on a farm in the beautiful Surrey countryside – with lots of stables!

Every sportsman or woman's wildest dream is to be asked to represent their country at the Olympics. So in 2000, when I was chosen for the Sydney Olympics, I was delighted. It was even more special to be part of the silver medal winning team.

Then, in 2003, I became the first (and only) person to win eventing's most coveted prize – the Rolex Grand Slam. The Grand Slam (winning three of the big events in a row – Badminton, Kentucky and Burghley) is the only three-day eventing slam in the sporting world.

2004 saw another Olympics and another call-up. Team GB performed brilliantly again and won another well-deserved silver medal, and I was lucky enough to win an individual bronze.

Having had several years without any top horses, I spent my time producing youngsters, so it was great in 2010 when one of those came through – Redesigned, a handsome chestnut gelding. In June that year I won my third

Bramham International Horse Trials title on Redesigned. We even managed a clear show jumping round in the pouring rain! By the end of 2010, Redesigned was on the squad for the World Championships in Kentucky where we finished fifth.

Today, as well as a hectic competition schedule, I'm also busy training horses for the future. At the Billy Stud, I work with my husband, William, and top breeder, Donal Barnwell, to produce top-class sport horses.

And in between all that I love writing the *Tilly's Pony Tails* books, and I'm also a trustee of World Horse Welfare, a fantastic charity dedicated to giving abused and neglected horses a second chance in life. For more information, visit their website at www.worldhorsewelfare.org.